If you [...] [wi]shes,
what would **YOU** wish for?

[j]ot them down here!

## MY WISH LIST*

1 _____
_____

2 _____
_____

3 _____
_____

*YOU <u>CAN'T</u> WISH FOR MORE WISHES,
SO DON'T EVEN BOTHER TRYING!

*Books by Steven Lenton*

GENIE AND TEENY: MAKE A WISH

*Coming soon*

GENIE AND TEENY: WISHFUL THINKING

# GENIE AND NIE TEENY

## MAKE A WISH

# Steven Lenton

HarperCollins *Children's Books*

First published in Great Britain by
HarperCollins *Children's Books* in 2021
HarperCollins *Children's Books* is a division of HarperCollins*Publishers* Ltd
HarperCollins Publishers
1 London Bridge Street
London SE1 9GF

www.harpercollins.co.uk

HarperCollins*Publishers*
1st Floor, Watermarque Building, Ringsend Road
Dublin 4, Ireland

1

ISBN 978–0–00–840820–6

Steven Lenton asserts the moral right to be identified as the author
and illustrator of the work.

A CIP catalogue record for this title is available from the British Library.

Printed and bound in England by CPI Group (UK) Ltd, Croydon, CR0 4YY

For Sallyanne Sweeney, who Made My Wishes Come true!
SLx

# HELLO, READER!

Welcome to a book chock-full of giggles, wishes, rude noises, old knickers and – best of all – GENIES!

Now, then, what do we know about genies? Well . . .

1. They are magical.
2. They live in lamps.
3. They make wishes come true.

Most genies are brilliant at granting wishes. Want a magical unicorn? **POOOF!** You got one!

Fancy a ride on the biggest roller coaster in the universe? **POOOF!** You're riding it!

Hungry and want beans on toast? **POOOF!** You're beans-on-toasting!

They can also help you in times of need . . .

Fed up with your unicorn and want a narwhal instead? **POOOF!** You're narwhalling!

About to be sick on the biggest roller coaster in the universe and want to get off? **POOOF!** You're free!

Burned your mouth on your beans on toast and need an ice cream to cool you down? **POOOF!** You're lickin'!

So, if you find an old lamp, it MIGHT be magical and it MIGHT just have a genie inside. Simply give it a rub to find out!

Rub here . . .

*Give it a go with this one . . . rub it with your finger . . . go on . . . and again . . . and again, then turn the page . . .*

**or rub here . . .**

**or even here . . .**

# TA-DAH!

Ah yes, I forgot to say. This lamp belongs to a genie called Grant. Grant loves a nap, so he's probably asleep (and snoring!), so you might have to knock quite loudly.

KNOCK!

KNOCK!

KNOCK!

Hmmm, still no joy.

Let's try shouting something like, 'OI, GRANT! WAKE UP!'

*Go on, give it a whirl!*

*One . . . two . . . three . . .*

'OI, GRANT! WAKE UP!'

Hooray! It worked!

This is Grant.

Hello, Grant – nice of you to join us.

Now Grant may LOOK like your average genie, and:

1. he IS magical . . .

2. he DOES live in a lamp BUT

3. he is NOT very good at making wishes . . .

For example – at Genie School, he once magicked up a **BORING IRON** instead of a **ROARING LION**. He conjured some **OLD SMELLY PANTS** instead of some **GOLD ELEPHANTS**, some **TINY WITCHES** instead of **SHINY RICHES**.

Once he even

created a **SNOT-**

**HAIRED BABOON**

instead of a **HOT-AIR BALLOON**,

which was VERY embarrassing.

Grant doesn't MEAN to be bad at making

wishes – he just gets his words a bit muddled.

And, as you'll see in the next chapter,

Grant makes his biggest mishap EVER . . .

# CHAPTER 1

# A RIGHT ROYAL MISTAKE

One day Grant was wandering past the royal palace when somehow the ruler of Genie World, Queen Mizelda, mistook him for the royal chef. He knew that he shouldn't have worn his chef hat that day, but all his other hats were in the wash.

Ah yes!

✻GENIE FACT ALERT!✻

**I should have mentioned –
Grant has an amazing collection
of hats that take pride of place
in his lamp – he uses different
hats for different occasions, as
you'll see later on ...**

'YOU THERE! CHEF GENIE!
TODAY IS MY BIRTHDAY AND I
WOULD LIKE A BIRTHDAY CAKE
FIT FOR A QUEEN, because,
ahem, **I AM THE QUEEN!**'

Despite trying to explain to the Queen that he wasn't the royal chef and that all his other hats were in the wash, Grant had a really good try at getting this very special and important wish right. He closed his eyes, concentrated and imagined the biggest, most fancy-pants cake he could think of. He wiggled his ears and fingers, he twiddled his nose . . . and he said his magic wishy word. (Every genie has a different magic wishy word, for example:

**ABRACADABRA,**

**ALAKAZAM** or PIFF PAFF POOF!

Your parents might have a favourite magic word too – 'PLEASE'. Can you guess what Grant's magic wishy word might be?)

Well, I bet you'll never guess.

Grant's magic wishy word is . . .

# Alaka-blam-a-bUMWhistle!

Yes, Grant shouted 'ALAKA-BLAM-A-BUMWHISTLE!' in front of Queen Mizelda, and instead of creating a fancy-pants birthday cake Grant turned her into a birthday SNAKE by mistake.

This was a BIG MIS-SNAKE!

The Queen was furioussssssssssss

and she banished him for good.

'HISS HISSSSSSSS HISSS HISS HISSSSSSSSSSS!'
the Queen hissed.

(Which means YOU ARE BANISHED FOR

GOOD in snake.)

And so Grant was

thrown out of

Genie World.

The lamp tumbled and fell through the sky, down through the clouds, hitting lots of things on the way.

**THUMP**

**THUD**

**DOOF**

**THUNK**

**SPLAT**

**CRASH**

*RUDE RASPBERRY SOUND!*

You get the idea.

The lamp eventually landed on Earth. In a park.

Grant blinked and looked around him. Inside the lamp, everything was higgledy-piggledy and topsy-turvy. His scatter cushions were scattered everywhere and Grant's belongings, including his impressive collection of nifty hats, were all over the place – **IT WAS A RIGHT MESS**.

Grant paused to take in everything that had just happened. He honestly hadn't meant to create all this havoc and felt a bit glum about it all. How would he get back to Genie World? In this sort of situation, he knew what to do, though. Without giving it a second thought, he searched around in the mess and eventually found what he was looking for – his Thinking Cap.

Now here's

## *ANOTHER GENIE FACT ALERT!*

**Grant's Thinking Cap is one of his most important hats because it helps him to**

**think calmly and carefully about what he needs to do next.**

He popped it on his head, closed his eyes and had a good long think . . .

In a few moments, Grant knew exactly what he needed to do. 'That's it! I need to find a way to get back in the Queen's good books – that way she'll let me return home. But first I need to check my lamp is okay. Thank you, Thinking Cap! You've done it again!'

Grant popped his head out of the top of the lamp and looked outside to inspect the damage.

The lamp was totally bashed and battered on the outside. The handle was bent, the spout was scratched and the lid was missing. It wasn't a pretty sight. He looked down and out and up the spout!

There was only one thing for it, Grant would have to look for a new place to live.

He packed up his belongings, then floated out of the lamp and into the park, keeping small and quiet.

## ✺YET ANOTHER GENIE FACT ALERT!✺

**Genies can morph into any shape and size whenever they like!** Grant thought it best to stay small and keep out of people's way until he knew more about his new environment. As he gazed around him, he could see birds and trees, although they weren't as colourful and magical-looking as the ones back in Genie World.

Next, he spotted a bird's nest in a tree. He floated up to it and snuggled inside. He was just starting to get comfy when suddenly a large bird swooped down and started trying to feed Grant some wriggly worms. Grant was very hungry by this stage, but he wasn't THAT hungry!

'I'm getting out of here. It's far too slimy,' he blurted, trying not to throw up.

Hmmm . . . and what was that over there? It looked like an old shoe . . . Maybe that would make a good new home? Quickly, he made his way over to it and jumped inside. It smelled like old cheese, it was a bit of a tight squeeze and there seemed to be something coming out of the top of it.

*Eurggh*, Grant thought to himself. It was a leg! A leg that belonged to someone, or something, very big. Very big and very hairy!

'This is too cramped and smelly,' moaned Grant as he squeezed out of the shoe with a crusty old toenail stuck to his bum.

Then he found a piece of old china.

'How fortunate! A lamp! What are the

chances of that?' Grant exclaimed.

It had a small crack, but a lovely

starry pattern all over the

outside and it

looked very

round and

cosy. You could

say it looked

TEA cosy.

'What a perfect lamp!

This is JUST RIGHT!' Grant

said, as he slid down the spout

and set about redecorating the inside.

He dusted his knick-knacks, polished his

potions and vacuumed his magic carpet.

Finally, he laid out his

prized collection

of hats.

When

everything was

looking shipshape,

Grant settled in for

the night.

He felt very sad about not being in Genie World with all the other genies, so he made himself a delicious hot chocolate piled high with marshmallows, chocolate sprinkles and smelly beans (he actually wanted jelly beans, but yet again his powers had failed him).

Then he read a chapter of his bedtime book,

which made him giggle-snort and cheered

him up no end.

What does a genie put in their cup of tea?

SUGAR LAMPS!

What is a genie's favourite takeaway?

WISH AND CHIPS!

And his favourite genie joke of all time:
What do you call a clever genie?

A GENIE-US!

Grant chuckled himself to sleep and, although he still felt sad, he was also hopeful that things would turn out okay. He also wished he was a genius.

# CHAPTER 2

# A NEW FURRY FRIEND

As Grant slept, he was dreaming of home and turning the genie Queen from a birthday snake back into a genie Queen when he was rudely awoken by a big slurpy licking sound, coming from outside his lamp!

# 'SLURP!'

'What was that?' exclaimed Grant as he was whisked up and out of the funnel in a cloud of smoke – someone must have rubbed the lamp and summoned him!

He looked around, but all he could see was darkness, so he popped back into his lamp and went straight to bed.

Grant started to dream again, this time about hot chocolate with JELLY not SMELLY beans on top, and he fell back to sleep.

Then he was woken up again by the large slurpy licking sound.

# 'SLUUUUUUURP!'

Again, Grant shot up out of the lamp in another puff of smoke.

## 'WHO'S THERE?'

he shouted into the pitch black, but he still couldn't see anything or anyone. He popped his helmet with a torch on his head and shone it around the park.

He looked left.

He looked right.

He looked up.

He looked down.

Then it started to rain. *Hmmm, what strange rain,* Grant thought to himself. *It's sort of yellow and doesn't smell particularly nice.*

He settled back into bed, but he really struggled to get back to sleep this time and decided to count flying carpets to help him doze off.

'One flying carpet . . . two flying carpets . . . three flying carpets . . .' And just as he got to 1,001 flying carpets and was very nearly asleep . . .

'SLUUUUUUUUUURP!'

Grant was summoned up in a third plume of smoke. 'OKAY! I'VE HAD ENOUGH! I'M TRYING TO GET TO SLEEP! HOW DARE YOU—' But Grant suddenly stopped shouting and started screaming. 'AAAAARRRRRRRRGGHHHH!'

There, right in front of him, was a huge, slobbery, hairy beast!

A drip of its drool landed on Grant's head.

'EURGH!' Grant shouted, wiping

away slobber.

The beast licked the side of Grant's face.

'LIIIIIIIIIIIIICK!'

Then he panted and smiled at Grant.

Grant realised the monster was friendly

after all. 'AWWW! You're actually quite

cute! I think you'd have eaten me

by now if you'd wanted to! What

do you wish for, O big, hairy,

slobbery one? I can grant you

three wishes!' exclaimed Grant

in his best and loudest genie voice.

'*Well, I can try to anyway,*' he added quietly.

The dog stared blankly at Grant and licked him again.

'Hmmm, okay.' Grant hopped on to the beast's head and gave him a good scratchin' behind his ears. 'Where did you come from, big fella?'

'BARK **BARK** BARKITY BARK!' the beast barked.

'Hmmm, that doesn't sound like genie language. I wonder what he's trying to tell me.'

'WOOF WOOF WOOFITY WOOF!' the beast woofed and pointed his tail towards a poster on a tree.

The poster read:

LOST PUPPY

ANSWERS TO THE
NAME 'TEENY'

REWARD
£500!

'OH!' Grant realised. 'You're lost and alone, like me! Hey, maybe I can help you to find your owner! I wonder why they named you Teeny, though – you're

MASSIVE!'

'It's too dark now, so let's go inside for a sleep and start our search in the morning when the sun comes up. At least it's stopped raining.'

Teeny tried to get inside the teapot with Grant, but it didn't go well . . .

He tried getting into the teapot paw-first.

Then he tried nose-first.

Then tail-first.

Maybe you could help to get Teeny to fit into the teapot (that Grant thinks is a lamp . . .)? *Try turning the book!*

No, that didn't work.

Maybe try *shaking it* to get Teeny inside?

Or maybe close the book and turn it upside *down* to shut him into the teapot . . . (But remember that you're on page 51!)

No, that didn't work either . . .

'Sorry, Teeny. You're way too big for this little lamp, which is DEFINITELY not a teapot. I'm afraid you'll have to sleep outside.'

Teeny looked sad and curled up round the teapot with a whimper.

# CHAPTER 3

# A TEENY MISSION

In the morning, the sun shone brightly on Grant and Teeny.

Grant jolted awake and wiped some sleepy slobber off the top of his head, unsure whether it was his or Teeny's.

Next (and this is one of the best things

about being a genie) he clicked his fingers

and in a magical flash he had . . .

**BRUSHED HIS HAIR**
(well, he does only
have three!)

**BRUSHED HIS TEETH**
(fortunately, he has more
than three of those!)

**HAD A SHOWER**
(genies get dirty too, you know!)

**AND GOT DRESSED!**

(Okay, he does only wear a waistcoat, so getting ready the normal way wouldn't take Grant THAT long, but how brilliant would it be to be able to get ready with just a click of your fingers?)

Then, Grant conjured up breakfast – sausages for Teeny and marshmallow ice cream for himself. Grant took his Explorer Hat off the shelf and popped it on his head.

Teeny had a quick wee and then they were both ready for their Teeny-owner finding mission . . .

# CHAPTER 4

# THE HUNT FOR TEENY'S OWNER

Grant scratched his head and wondered where to look first.

He took his binoculars out from under his hat and had a good look around the park. 'I think, because you are so **BIG**, we are looking for quite a **BIG** person, a **BIG** person probably holding a dog lead. A **BIG** person probably holding a dog lead and probably crying because they are so sad that they can't find you. Now let's see . . .'

Grant spotted a clown. 'Hmm, this person is **BIG,** but he looks far too happy.'

Then he spied someone else. 'Now this person has a LEAD, but they already have something at the end of it. Aww, they look really SAD . . . Oh, but I don't think it's a person!'

Grant sighed heavily.

'I don't think your owner is in the park, Teeny. We'll just have to search somewhere else . . .'

'RIBBIT!'

# CHAPTER 5
# EXPLORING TOWN

Grant and Teeny toddled off to town.

This was Grant's first visit to Earth so he

was in awe of everything he saw. It all looked

like it did in the books he had studied at

Genie School, but it was SO much bigger

and even more amazing in real life.

When Grant saw something he remembered from his GUIDE TO EARTHLY EARTHLINGS, he couldn't help but shout it out excitedly as he walked past them.

'A LOUD MAN WHO CAN'T SING!'

'A FLYING RAT!'

'A FAKE WOBBLY STATUE!'

'A NAKED LADY!'

Grant was causing quite a stir in town . . .

Fortunately, just in the nick of time, Teeny got a whiff of something delicious and sped off round a corner.

'**Whoa**, slow down, Teeny!' shouted Grant as they followed the delicious whiffy trail.

Teeny skidded to a halt as the trail ended at a hot-dog stand. Teeny could never resist a sausage, and grabbed an entire string of them.

'OI, YOU MANGEY LITTLE MUTT!'

The hot-dog-stand owner shouted and grabbed Teeny by the collar. He was VERY angry indeed and looked as if he was about to get EVEN angrier, but the sound of an engine screeching to a halt stopped him in his tracks.

Then there was a BOOF! and something hit him on the head . . .

# CHAPTER 6

# A STRANGE OLD LADY

'YOU NASTY SAUSAGEY MAN! *Being mean to my gorgeous little puppy-poo!'*

Grant and Teeny looked up and saw an old lady dressed from head to toe in purple, clutching a now slightly bent umbrella. She started to cry. *'Sob, sob! I've been looking all over for you! Sob, sob!'*

Grant jumped into the teapot, not wanting to get in the way of this heartwarming reunion, but peered through a small gap under the teapot lid as the old lady gave Teeny a huge hug and covered him in kisses.

Teeny looked shocked – he seemed unsure of who this lady was. She smelled of an odd mix of lavender, toffees and wet dog.

'Oh, where have you been, my DARLING DOODLE-DUMPLING? Mummy's missed you!'

A little tear of homesickness rolled down Grant's cheek. He had been so involved in helping Teeny that he had forgotten how much he was missing home himself.

The old lady popped Teeny in her handbag next to a packet of super-sticky, sticky toffees. 'Let's get you home. You must be starving! And – OOOOOH! – you have a gorgeous little teapot! Hmmm, a shame that it's yellow, but I'll take it with me anyway.'

'Teapot?' Grant huffed. 'This is a lamp, not a teapot! And what's wrong with yellow?'

'What was that little squeaky sound?' the old lady asked sharply. 'Whoops! I must have had too many toffees!'

Then she waddled along the road and plonked herself on to a purple moped parked on the roadside. She put Teeny and her handbag containing the teapot on the seat in the sidecar, revved the engine and sped off in a cloud of smoke.

# CHAPTER 7

# THE OLD LADY'S HOUSE

After some scarily skiddy driving and a touch of travel sickness, they arrived at the old lady's house.

Grant tried to get out of the teapot by pushing the lid open, but it was stuck. He

tried the spout, but that seemed to be blocked too!

The old lady's super-sticky toffees must have fallen out of the packet and stuck to the outside, so he couldn't escape.

Can you help Grant? Maybe you could try to get the toffees off the teapot!

Try wiping them off . . . ?

*Or shake the book again to get rid of them?*

No? Okay, well, thank you for trying.

Grant could JUST about see through the small crack in the side of the teapot and he noticed that the old lady's house was very, erm . . . PURPLE.

The roof was purple, the walls were purple, the front door was purple. Even the flowers in the garden were ALL purple.

'Gosh, your owner really likes purple, eh, Teeny!' he whispered.

'In you go, my darling doggy!' the old lady said, pushing Teeny into her living room.

Teeny and Grant's mouths dropped wide open when they saw the inside of the house.

Not only was the outside of her house purple, the entire INSIDE of her house was purple too: purple furniture, purple paintings, purple lights, purple wallpaper and even purple DOGS – wait, rewind –

# WHAT?

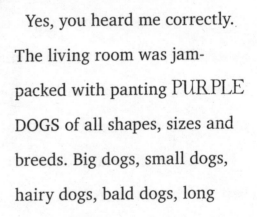

Yes, you heard me correctly. The living room was jam-packed with panting PURPLE DOGS of all shapes, sizes and breeds. Big dogs, small dogs, hairy dogs, bald dogs, long

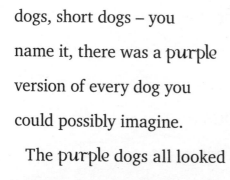

dogs, short dogs – you
name it, there was a purple
version of every dog you
could possibly imagine.

The purple dogs all looked
at Teeny and blinked.

The old lady slammed the door behind them and clapped her hands with glee. 'Hee hee! At last, I, Lavinia Lavender, have found the last dog for my collection!' she cackled.

Grant gulped. 'Oh, Teeny! Maybe this isn't your owner after all!'

Teeny looked at Grant with a sort of 'DUH!' expression and shook his head.

Before they could escape, the old lady grabbed a dog cage, put Teeny inside it and locked the door.

'**YELP!**' yelped Teeny.

'Don't worry! I'll get you out of there, fella!' Grant whispered.

But Grant wasn't quite sure how – he was quite literally **STUCK** inside the teapot. He HEAVED and he PUSHED, he **PULLED** and he tugged.

*They must be the stickiest toffees in the world,* thought Grant.

The other dogs all cowered in a corner – they knew what was going to happen next . . .

## CHAPTER 8
# PUPPY PURPLEFICATION

The old lady went to her kitchen and popped the purple kettle on. 'Now where is that new teapot? Aha, there it is.'

'She's going to fill my lovely new lamp,

that is **NOT** a teapot, with boiling water!'
Grant panicked. 'And I can't swim!'

Lavinia picked up the teapot and it stuck to her hands.

'Yuck!' she shouted as she noticed it had toffees stuck to the lid and down the spout. She gave it a shake to try to get it all off. (*But we know that doesn't work, don't we?*)

'I haven't got time to clean this now. I'll sort it out later,' she said, and she popped it back into her handbag.

Grant wiped his brow and sighed in relief.

Lavinia went back to the kitchen, filled her old purple teapot with water and put a purple tea cosy on it. She put a teacake in the purple toaster and when it was ready she smothered it in purple jam and poured her tea into a purple cup and saucer.

Next, she put an old record on her old purple record player, switched it on and started doing a funny dance that made her look like a prancing purple peacock.

The purple dogs all looked at each other and gulped.

She started singing along to the tune of 'I Can Sing a Rainbow', but she was more out of tune than a constipated cuckoo and she changed all the lyrics so it went a bit like this:

*Purple and purple and purple and purple,*

*Purple and purple and purple,*

*I can sing a rainbow . . .*

*Sing a rainbow!*

Then she opened a door to another purple room that looked like a hair salon, and in the centre of the room was a large shape covered in a big purple sheet.

'Okay, my fluffy new friend, time for a makeover, or as I, Lavinia Lavender, Lavvy to my friends –' *I bet she hasn't got many of those*, Grant thought to himself – 'like to call it,

# *PUPPY PURPLEFICATION!'*

She whipped off the cover to reveal a funny-looking contraption with a conveyor belt and a big sign above it:

# THE PATENT-PENDING PUPPY PURPLEFICATION MACHINE

'AT LAST, LAVINIA LAVENDER'S PACK OF *PURPLE* PERFORMING POOCHES IS COMPLETE!' Lavinia announced.

'I have waited years for this moment, and now I'm finally ready to beat my old rival DARCEY DAVENPORT AND HER DISCO-DANCING DALMATIANS in the BIG DANCING DOG SHOW!'

She took Teeny out of the cage, plonked him on the conveyor belt and pressed the big green **START** button. The machine shook

HAIRCUT

FUR
DYE

and whirred as Teeny was taken through the purplefication process. Grant looked on, helpless.

After a few moments, the machine coughed, spluttered and made a rather rude raspberry sound – and then Teeny appeared at the other end.

NAIL POLISH

BLOW DRY

'*TA-DAAAAAAAAH! PURPLE PUPPY PERFECTION!*' exclaimed Lavinia Lavender.

Teeny looked like a purple powder puff!

Grant couldn't help but let out a little giggle at seeing Teeny looking so funny.

'*Oooh, wait! I forgot the finishing touch!*' shrieked Lavinia. Grant dreaded to think how much MORE silly she was going to make Teeny look, and he stared in horror as Lavinia put a **GINORMOUS** sparkly purple bow in Teeny's fur.

'Time to rehearse our award-winning show!'

# CHAPTER 9

# REHEARSAL!

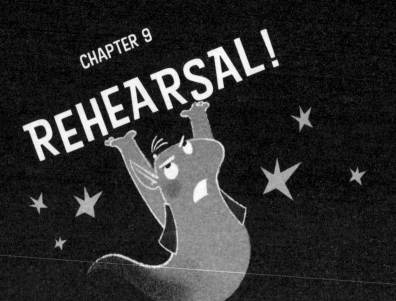

Grant tried to open the lid of the teapot a bit more, but the sticky toffees were still stuck there, and it just wouldn't budge!

Maybe you could try to help him by shaking the teapot again? *Go on, give it a go!*

Still no joy – they really are **SUPER**-sticky.
Let's try again later . . .

Lavinia put the rainbow song on the record player again, clapped her hands **VERY** loudly and called,

'PURPLE PUPS, PERFORM!'

and the dogs all leapt into action, doing a bizarre routine with Lavinia clapping to the beat. 'And you, new dog,' she said, pointing at Teeny, 'follow them perfectly!'

Teeny gulped and did his best to copy everything the dogs did.

They posed.

They pedalled.

They piled.

They paraded.

They preened, pirouetted and perspired.

They performed, performed, **PERFORMED!**

Teeny was exhausted, but just about managed to keep up with the other dogs.

'Well done, my darlings. Now it's time for bed. We all need our beauty sleep!' (*Some more than others*, Grant thought.) 'Tomorrow is MY, er . . . I mean, OUR big day!'

Lavinia tucked all the dogs into a large dog bed and kissed each one goodnight, naming them as she did so.

'Goodnight, Poopsie Pie. Sweet dreams, Peachy Poo. Nighty-night, Pickle Pots. Bonsoir, Poopsie Doopsie. Sleep tight, Plumpy Pants. Goodnight, Puddle Pumpkin. Night-night, Puffle Pops, and, ah . . . my new recruit! Now what shall I call you . . . I know, you look like a BARRY to me! Goodnight, BARRY!'

Teeny looked at the lamp that was NOT a teapot and Grant whispered through the teapot that was not a lamp, 'Don't worry, BARRY! I'll get us out of here!'

Lavinia picked up her handbag with the teapot still inside it, turned off the light and locked the door behind her.

## CHAPTER 10
# A STICKY SITUATION!

Lavinia walked up the stairs humming her song again. It was even worse than before – she sounded like an old guitar with strings made of mouldy cheese.

She got to her bedroom and sat on her bed.

'Ooooh, what a day it's been,' she chuckled to herself. She took her teeth out of her mouth and plopped them in a glass of water on her bedside table.

'EWW, GROSS!' shouted Grant, who, peering through the teapot crack, was nearly sick at the sight.

'*Who's there?*' Lavinia shouted, jumping off the bed. '*Show yourself!*'

Grant clapped his hands over his mouth so he would not make another sound.

Lavinia checked under the bed, in her wardrobe and her knicker drawer, just in case. 'Hmm, must just be the wind,' she said, shrugging her shoulders, and she sat back down on the bed.

She opened her handbag and reached in to get a sticky toffee. As she pulled one out the teapot came with it!

'What's this? Ah, yes, the new doggy had this teapot in its mouth when I snatched, er . . . I mean, when I SAVED it this afternoon. What a funny-looking thing,

chipped, dusty and sticky, but maybe with a
bit of spit and polish it will look quite snazzy.'

She went back to her knicker drawer, took
out a pair of old frilly pants, spat on the
teapot and rubbed . . .

# POOOF!!!

A **big** cloud of smoke shot out of the spout and Grant appeared, still holding his hands over his mouth and, somehow, wearing Lavinia's knickers. He looked down at her and did an embarrassed little wave.

'Good 'eavens, it's a . . . a . . . GENIE!' she screamed, and fainted to the floor with a flop.

Grant flew down to her face to check if she was still breathing – she definitely was! Her breath stank of mouldy old Brussel sprouts.

Her eyes opened slowly. 'What a funny dream. I thought I saw a . . . a . . . a . . . *AAAAAAAAAARGH! GENIE!'* she screamed as she saw Grant waving at her, then she fainted again.

She woke up a second time, sat up, popped her teeth back in, then picked up the glass of water, threw it in her own face and stared at Grant.

'I can't believe there's a GENIE in my room! Now, is it true what they say about being given three wishes?'

# CHAPTER 11

# LAVINIA'S THREE WISHES

'Yes, it's true,' replied Grant. 'Because you rubbed the lamp with your big old flowery knickers, you are entitled to three wishes.'

'Now, let me see, what do I fancy? Hmmm, I can't think of anything and, rats, I'm out of toffees. Chewing toffees always helps me think. I wish I had a lifetime supply of sticky toffees so I'd never run out again.'

'Your wish is my command!' said Grant. He closed his eyes, swirled his hands in the air and said his magic wishy word,

'Alaka-blam-a-buMwhistle!' and *POOOF!*

'*WHAT?*' cried Lavinia. 'I didn't make a wish!'

'Yes, you did!' Grant replied.

Lavinia shrieked as she stared around the

room. She was surrounded by mountains of cups and mugs full of browny-green-goo. She picked up one of the cups and sniffed it.

'*EURRRGH!* This smells like SICK!' She held her nose, took a sip and then spat out a mouthful of the chunky liquid.

'This is sicky coffee, you idiot! I said a lifetime supply of STICKY TOFFEE, not SICKY COFFEE! I HATE COFFEE! Especially coffee made from sick!'

Grant gulped and felt rather embarrassed, but also wanted to have a bit of a giggle at the sight of Lavinia jumping up and down in a rage.

'What on earth am I going to do with it all? And I didn't even wish for this! GRRR! I wish I hadn't even mentioned sticky toffees!' Then Lavinia gasped, realising what she'd done!

With an 'Alaka-blam-a-bumwhistle!.' the sicky coffees vanished without a trace and the room was back to normal. (Well, apart from it still being entirely purple.)

Grant was quite astonished – he'd actually sort of got a wish right!

But Lavinia was fuming! She was so cross that her face went bright red and smoke shot out of her ears.

'I demand more wishes – no! I WISH FOR MORE WISHES, YOU STUPID GENIE! NOOOOW!'

'I'm ever so sorry, Miss Lavender,' said Grant, 'but it's a genie rule that you can't actually wish for more wishes. Look . . .'

Grant took his *Genie Handbook* out from under his hat and found the right page to show her.

# GENIE RULE NUMBER 7

Under no circumstances, and no matter how desperate or angry your master becomes, you must NEVER grant them more than three wishes.

'*WHAT?*' screeched Lavinia. '*It was your fault that I wasted two wishes! What kind of genie ARE you?*'

'Not a very good one, I'm afraid. I was kicked out of Genie World because I'm so hopeless at making wishes. Sorry.' Grant was SORT of sorry, but also quite glad that the wish hadn't gone according to plan this time because he really did not like Lavinia Lavender. Not one bit.

'*Now* you tell me!' said Lavinia, rolling her eyes. 'Well, I have ONE wish left, so I'd better make it a good one. Aha! I know! Genie, I wish to win the BIG DANCING DOG

SHOW! *And beat Darcey Davenport and her Disco-dancing Dalmatians!*' she shrieked at Grant, and with a cheeky wink he said his magic wishy word,

'Alaka-blam-a-buMwhistle!'

and in a huge puff of smoke they were transported to the

# BIG DANCING DOG SHOW!

Lavinia looked around excitedly as she saw all her rivals.

There was . . .

Percy Perfect and his
Prancing Preeny Poodles . . .

Walter Wiggybottom and
his Waltzing Whippets . . .

1·2·3    1·2·3

and, of course, there, looking incredibly smug, was Darcey Davenport, singing and stretching with her Disco-dancing Dalmatians.

'Ha ha! They haven't a chance against me and my gorgeous – oh, Genie! Where are my perfect purple pooches?'

'Ah, well . . .' Grant started to reply, but at that moment all the other entrants turned to look at Lavinia and burst into laughter.

'WHAT? What are you all gawping at?' she screamed.

Darcey Davenport walked up to her with a large mirror and Lavinia shrieked in horror.

'*WOOF! WOOF BARK BARK WOOF SNAAAAAARL?!*' which means, '*AAAAARGH! GENIE, WHAT HAVE YOU DONE?*'

Grant had turned Lavinia into a big purple dog with paws, ears and a tail!

'You said YOU wanted to win the BIG DANCING DOG SHOW! So here you are!' he giggled.

Before she had chance to reply, her intro

music of 'I Can Sing a Rainbow' began and
Lavinia leapt into the spotlight. She tried
to dance and sing, but because she was on
four legs with a tail getting in the way she
kept falling over, looking incredibly silly.

Also, because she could only woof and bark instead of sing, Lavinia sounded even more terrible than usual! The audience couldn't believe what they were seeing and literally howled with laughter.

At the end of her performance, the room fell silent. Lavinia was embarrassed and angry, and snarled at Grant, who gulped. But her anger soon changed to bemusement when at the award ceremony she was crowned BEST IN SHOW!

'*Bark, bark, woof woofity woof woof, barkity bark bark, woof woof bark,*' she said, which translated into human means, '*WOW! Thank you, everyone. I'd like to thank my friends, my opponents for being so terrible, my genie, but mainly myself for being so phenomenally talented.*'

The audience was flabbergasted.

Lavinia looked down at the trophy

and noticed the small print

BEST IN SHOW*
*for looking really stupid!

on the engraving. She was immediately

furious again and screamed, '*BARK BARK*

*WOOF BAAAAAAAAAAAAARK!*'

which translated into human means,

*'GENIIIIIIIIIIIEEEEEEEEEE!'*

Grant quickly clicked his fingers and with another big puff of smoke he and Lavinia disappeared.

# CHAPTER 12

# THE PURPLE POOCHES' REVENGE

All the dogs woke up with a start and looked stunned when Grant and Lavinia appeared in a puff of smoke back in the living room. Teeny was so pleased to see Grant that he did a little bit of a wee, then

bounded over and gave Grant a big, slobbery
lick on the side of his face.

Grant smiled and gave Teeny a big hug
in return.

Then all the dogs looked at Lavinia and growled. Lavinia yelped and made a run for it, dashing straight for the door, but it was still locked! The key was on her collar, but she now had paws rather than hands!

She ran towards the PATENT-PENDING PUPPY PURPLEFICATION MACHINE and leapt on to the conveyor belt.

The dogs all watched as the machine whirred into action and Lavinia was **pulled** and PUMMELLED through each stage of the purplefication process.

Because she landed on the machine upside down, she appeared at the other end of the conveyor belt with a rather bald and quite beautifully styled bottom!

The dogs and Grant all sniggered at Lavinia's new look.

Grant saw his opportunity, grabbed the key from her collar, flew to the door and unlocked it. All the dogs ran excitedly out of the living room and front door, each of them licking Grant as they ran past. They were free at last!

Well done, Grant! You saved the day and
taught that silly old Lavinia Lavender a thing
or two!

The dogs all ran home to their owners and the police arrived to deal with Lavinia (although, funnily enough, they never found her).

Teeny didn't run off. He was still ownerless, but at least he had Grant. They were both alone, but they were alone together.

# CHAPTER 13

# SHELTER

Grant and Teeny left Lavinia's house behind and headed back out into the world. They wandered down the road and along a deserted shopping street.

'I know we need to find your owner, Teeny,'

said Grant, 'but let's find some shelter first. It's starting to get dark and the sky looks a bit threatening and stormy.'

Grant was right! Just then, thunder and lightning began, so they stopped to rest underneath a shop canopy.

Grant said goodnight to Teeny and gave him a good scratch under his chin. 'Don't worry, boy. I know we'll find your owner soon.' And Grant was right AGAIN because at that moment they heard voices calling in the distance.

'Mum . . . I think it's . . . YES! TEENY! It IS you!'

Teeny's ears pricked up and he began wagging his tail. There, running towards him under an umbrella, were a little girl and her mum – his owners! Grant flew inside the teapot, not wanting to disturb this REAL family reunion, and watched through the spout.

'We found you at last!' they shouted as they scooped him up into their arms and gave him the biggest hug he'd ever had. 'Oh, where have you been and, er, why do you have a yellow teapot?'

'Erm, I think you'll find it's a LAMP,' whispered Grant, dabbing a tear from his eye.

'What was that noise?' said Mum. Grant quickly made a lightning sound with his mouth. 'Gosh, this storm really is dreadful. Let's get you home safe and warm.'

The little girl held Teeny and off they walked. Teeny looked over the girl's shoulder at Grant, who was sadly waving goodbye.

Teeny started to whimper loudly.

'Aw, what's wrong, Teeny? Don't worry! We're here now,' the girl replied, patting him gently on the head. But Teeny barked, jumped from her arms and sped towards the teapot.

Mum looked puzzled. 'What is it, Teeny?' she asked. 'You, er, you want us to take this home too?'

'Bark, bark, bark . . .' barked Teeny.

'Oh, all right. Why not?' And Mum picked up the teapot as Teeny jumped back into the little girl's arms.

Grant popped his head out of the teapot.

'Thank you, Teeny,' he said, and gave him a little wink.

*

When they got home, Mum put the teapot on the kitchen table, dried Teeny with a hairdryer and gave him some fresh water and a big bowl of food.

'We are so glad you're back, little one,' they said as they kissed him on the forehead and popped him in his basket on the kitchen floor. 'Now get a good night's sleep and we will see you first thing in the morning. You must be pooped!'

As they left the room and went upstairs to

bed, Teeny opened one eye to make sure the coast was clear. Then he jumped up on to the table to check on Grant, who was sitting on the teapot waiting for him.

'Teeny, we found your owners and they are lovely! AND you brought me home with you! Thank you so much . . .' and he gave Teeny the smallest but nicest hug Teeny had ever had. 'They are right, though. Let's get a good night's sleep. I'm more tired than an old pair of Lavinia Lavender's knickers!'

Teeny remembered what had happened the night before when he'd tried to get into Grant's not-a-teapot lamp, so he curled up round it and drifted off to sleep.

Grant looked at Teeny and realised it couldn't be nice for him to be sleeping on the kitchen table, so he decided to do something a little bit naughty . . .

Now, as we have discovered in this story, there are a few rules when it comes to granting wishes and it's rather important to try to stick to them as best you can, but SOMETIMES you have to bend the rules a little. And that's exactly what Grant is about to do . . .

# CHAPTER 14

# THE FINAL WISH

Because Teeny can't talk, Grant thought it would be all right to GUESS a wish for him. Do you think that would be okay? Yes, I do too – JUST this once!

Grant was pretty certain that Teeny would

wish to be all tucked up and cosy inside the lamp right now.

So Grant closed his eyes, focused on making Teeny teeny tiny, clicked his fingers and whispered his magic wishy word:

'Alaka-blam-a-bumWhistle!'

With a flash of light, Grant opened his eyes, but instead of making Teeny tiny enough to fit inside the lamp, he had turned Teeny an unusual GREENY colour instead!

'Whoops! I'd better try again,' sighed Grant.

He closed his eyes, focused on Teeny,

clicked his fingers and whispered,

'Alaka-blam-a-
bumwhistle!'

Grant cautiously opened one eye . . . 'OH

NO, I'VE DONE IT AGAIN!'

Teeny now looked like one of Grant's hats,

the one like a cap but with a little propellor

on top – a BEANIE!

*I'll have one more go,* Grant thought nervously. *I HAVE to get it right this time.*

Grant stretched his arms, took a big, deep breath and shook his head from side to side to loosen up.

He closed his eyes, he really, REALLY concentrated (like he sometimes does when he does a big poo) and confidently said his magic wishy word . . .

# 'Alaka-blam-a-buMwhistle!'

There was a flash of light, then . . . silence.

Grant didn't dare open his eyes, and kept

them tightly shut.

Then he heard a very small 'woof woof'.

He opened his eyes and there in front of him was Teeny!

'TEENY! Now you really ARE teeny, Teeny!'

Teeny leapt into Grant's arms and licked the side of his face.

'I think I chose the right wish for you, Teeny. What do you think?' said Grant, giving Teeny a really good scratch behind his teeny Teeny ears.

Teeny licked Grant's face. 'Hee hee, that tickles, Teeny,' giggled Grant.

He clicked his fingers
and – **PUFF!** – they

were both in the warmth of his

cosy not-a-teapot.

Grant reached behind his pillow and pulled

out his favourite book . . .

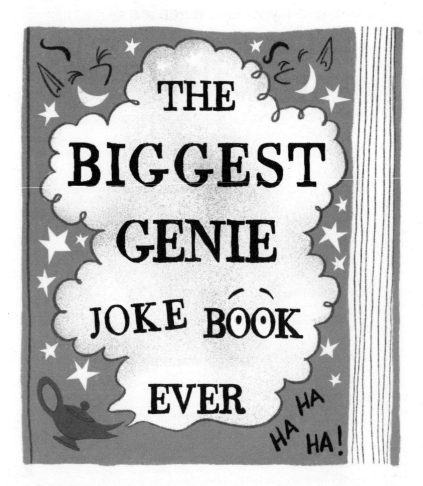

and told Teeny a bedtime joke.

'What do you call a genie's dog?

An abracalabrador!'

Teeny just yawned, unimpressed.

He curled up in Grant's arms and the two
of them drifted off to sleep, dreaming about
their next magical adventure . . .

'Goodnight, Teeny, or should I say BARRY!'
chuckled Grant. *Now, let's help them go to
sleep by saying goodnight to them both. Close
this book carefully . . .*

'Goodnight, Genie

and Teeny . . .'

# HOW TO DRAW GRANT THE GENIE

**1**

Draw a curvy line to make a nose shape.

**2** Then a 'J' shape for his back...

**3** And a curvy line to make his tummy and tail.

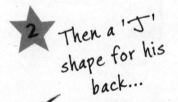

**4**

Then draw two circles for the eyes and two lines for the eyebrows.

Add two more circles and colour them in to make his pupils, then add his smiley mouth and hair!

**5**

**6**

Next, draw his pointy ear and one of his arms.

**7**

Draw his waistcoat round his arm and next to his tummy.

**8**

Draw his waving arm next.

**9**

Finally, colour him in and maybe add one of his favourite hats!

DRAW YOUR GENIE HERE!

>lease share your drawings on social media using #GenieandTeeny

STEVEN LENTON is a multi-award-winning illustrator, originally from Cheshire, now working from his studios in Brighton and London with his French bulldog, Big-Eared Bob!

He has illustrated many children's books, including *Head Kid* and *Future Friend* by David Baddiel, *The Hundred and One Dalmatians* adapted by Peter Bently, The Shifty McGifty and Slippery Sam series by Tracey Corderoy, Frank Cottrell-Boyce's fiction titles and Steven Butler's Sainsbury's Prize-winning The Nothing to See Here Hotel series.

He has illustrated two World Book Day titles and regularly appears at literary festivals, live events and schools across the UK.

Steven has his own Draw-Along-A-Lenton YouTube channel, showing you how to draw a range of his characters, and he was in the Top 20 Bookseller Bestselling Illustrator Chart 2019.

*Genie and Teeny* is Steven's first foray into children's fiction and he really hopes you have enjoyed Grant and Teeny's first adventure!

Find out more about Steven and his work at stevenlenton.com.